ARCHIE

Bloomsbury Publishing, London, New Delhi, New York and Sydney

First published in Great Britain in 2012 by Bloomsbury Publishing Plc
50 Bedford Square, London, WC1B 3DP

This paperback edition first published in 2013 by Bloomsbury Publishing Plc

A CIP catalogue record for this book is available from the British Library

ISBN 978 1 4088 2862 5 (HB)
ISBN 978 1 4088 2864 9 (PB)

Printed in China by C&C Offset Printing Co, Shenzhen, Guangdong

1 3 5 7 9 10 8 6 4 2

www.bloomsbury.com
www.domenicamoregordon.com

ARCHIE

Domenica More Gordon

BLOOMSBURY

LONDON   NEW DELHI   NEW YORK   SYDNEY

zzzzzz

pom pom pom de pom...

RIN

RING

RING

RING

RING